The City ABC Book

For my mother, who has taught me to see.
For my daughter, who I hope I can teach to see.

— Z.M.

Photographs © 2001 Zoran Milich

Kids Can Press acknowledges the financial support of the Ontario Arts Council, the Canada Council for the Arts and the Government of Canada, through the BPIDP, for our publishing activity.

Published in Canada by
Kids Can Press Ltd.
29 Birch Avenue
Toronto, ON M4V 1E2

Published in the U.S. by
Kids Can Press Ltd.
2250 Military Road
Tonawanda, NY 14150

www.kidscanpress.com

The text is set in Futura.

Designed by Karen Birkemoe
Printed and bound in Hong Kong, China, by Book Art Inc., Toronto

The hardcover edition of this book is smyth sewn casebound.
The paperback edition of this book is limp sewn with a drawn-on cover.

CM 01 0 9 8 7 6 5 4 3 2
CM PA 02 0 9 8 7 6 5 4 3 2

National Library of Canada Cataloguing in Publication Data

Milich, Zoran
        The city ABC book

ISBN 1-55074-942-0 (bound).
ISBN 1-55074-948-X (pbk.).

1. English language — Alphabet — Juvenile literature. 2. Cities and towns — Pictorial works — Juvenile literature. I. Title.

PE1155.M554 2001   j421'.1   C00-932107-1

Kids Can Press is a *Corus*™ Entertainment company

The City ABC Book

by ZORAN MILICH

Kids Can Press

Aa

BUSINESS HOURS

MONDAY	CLOSED
TUESDAY	10:00-6:00
WEDNESDAY	10:00-6:00
THURSDAY	10:00-9:00
FRIDAY	10:00-6:00
SATURDAY	10:00-6:00
SUNDAY	12:00-5:00

Bb

Cc

Dd   Ee

Ff

Gg

Hh

Ii

Jj

Kk   Ll

Mm

Nn Oo

Pp

Qq

Rr

Ss

Tt

Uu

Vv

Ww

Yy   Zz